How Many Fish?

MY FIRST
I Can Read Book®

How Many Fish?

story by **Caron Lee Cohen**
pictures by **S. D. Schindler**

HarperCollins*Publishers*

HarperCollins®, 🕮®, and I Can Read Book®
are trademarks of HarperCollins Publishers Inc.

How Many Fish?
Text copyright © 1998 by Caron Lee Cohen
Illustrations copyright © 1998 by S. D. Schindler
Manufactured in China. All rights reserved.
For information address HarperCollins Children's Books, a division of
HarperCollins Publishers, 195 Broadway, New York, NY 10007.
www.harpercollins.com

First Harper Trophy edition, 2000
❖
Visit us on the World Wide Web!
http://www.harperchildrens.com
14 15 16 17 SCP 21

For Ruth Stern,
who knows how many fish it takes.
—C.L.C.

How many fish?

How many fish?

Six little fish in the bay.

Where do they go?
Why do they go?

8

Six little fish on their way.

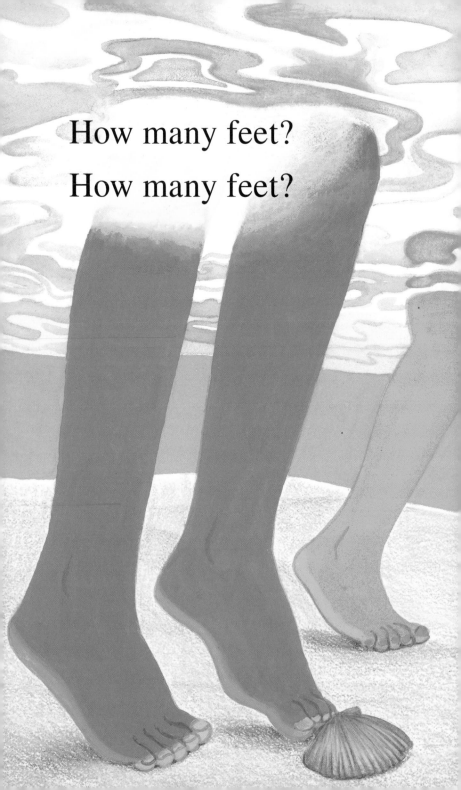

How many feet?

How many feet?

Six little feet in the bay.

Where do they go?

Why do they go?

Six little feet on their way.

13

How many fish?

How many fish?

One yellow fish in the bay.

Where's yellow fish?

Where's yellow fish?

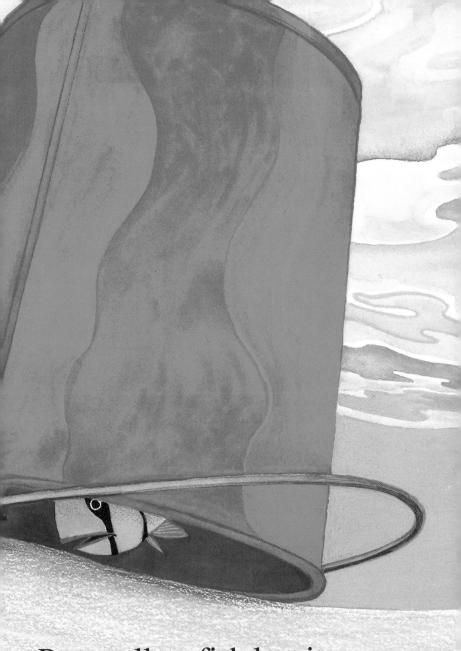

Poor yellow fish lost its way.

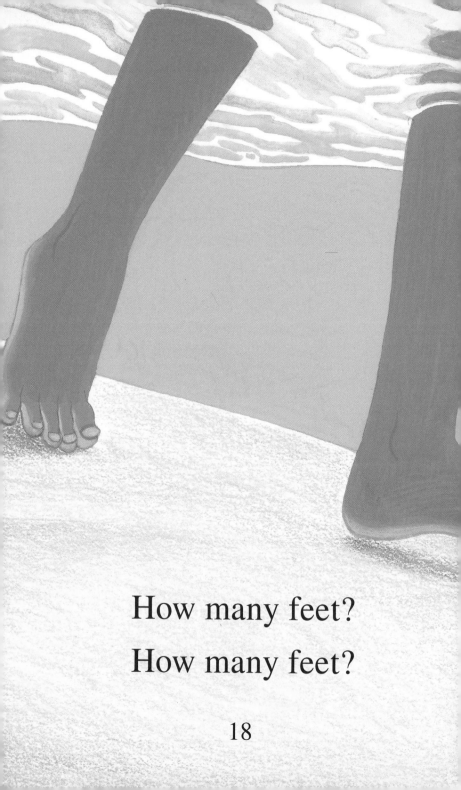

How many feet?
How many feet?

Two little feet in the bay.

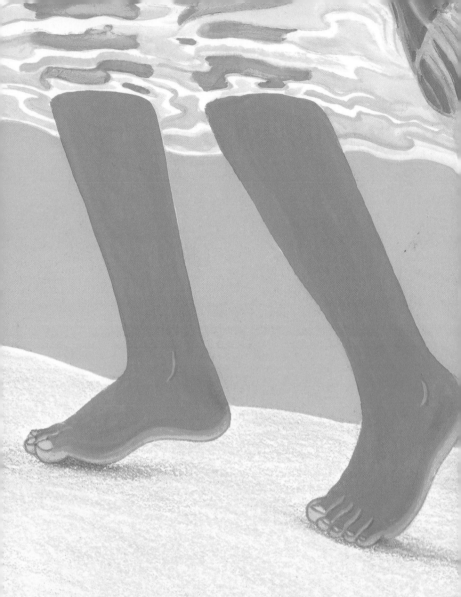

Where's the red pail?

Where's the red pail?

Two little feet dash away.

One happy fish.

One happy fish.

One happy fish on its way!

How many fish?

How many fish?

Six little fish in the bay!